TOUGH TED
AND THE TALE OF THE TATTERED EAR

Simon Bond

FANTAIL

The Fairwinds Café was quiet, so Tough and Desmond decided to tidy up the place. After a while, they stopped to catch their breath. They did not say anything for a moment, then Tough looked across and out of the window. He noticed a figure looking at the menu.

"Howling hurricanes!" gasped Tough with a start. "I don't believe my eyes!"

"What's up, Tough?" asked Desmond, a little surprised. "What's wrong?"

"Well, nothing for the moment, Desmond, but that might change…" Tough answered quietly.

"What do you mean?" Desmond asked, somewhat confused.

"Do you see that man outside?" said Tough, pointing. Desmond nodded. "It's because of him that I have this." He touched his torn ear.

"What? Your tattered ear?" Desmond said. "Did he do it? Did you have a fight with him?"

"Well, it wasn't really a fight," said Tough, sounding thoughtful. "Actually, I saved his life – I saved Sneaky McQueen."

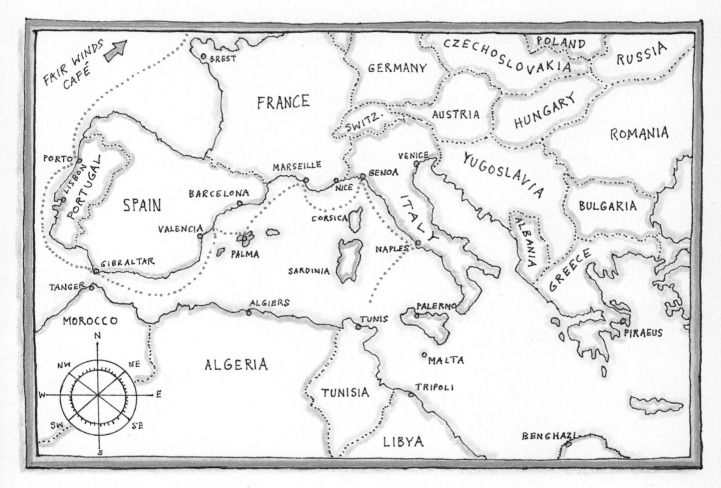

Desmond had always wondered how his friend had come by the big nick in his left ear and moved closer to listen to Tough's story. Tough took a deep breath.

"It started like this," he began. "Many years ago when I was quite young, I was part of the crew of a small freighter sailing around the Mediterranean from port to port. It wasn't very exciting … just carrying this here, that there … normal, ordinary cargo work."

"The most interesting thing to happen was the occasional storm, but our little ship was as tough as my beard. She could take anything the weather threw at her – and a bucketful more!"

"We didn't have a big crew, but we did have a steward who basically looked after us … cooking, cleaning, laundry …"

"Shoe polishing?" piped in Desmond.

"Shoe polishing ..." continued Tough, "and anything else we needed. That steward was Sneaky McQueen, and somehow I just didn't trust him. He always seemed to be popping out of cabins or into shadows. Very odd – but nothing you could put your finger on."

"So what happened next?" asked an eager Desmond.

"There was nothing to begin with ... just a funny feeling I had about the bloke. We chugged around for a few weeks docking every day or so for cargo and supplies. Sometimes I would go ashore with some of my shipmates, but mostly it was only Sneaky who visited the ports."

"He always seemed to have a parcel to mail home. I thought that a little bit odd. We all sent postcards and presents home to someone from time to time, of course, but not from every port of call. Some of the lads reckoned he might have a sweetheart back home, but he didn't seem the type to me."

"Why, was he ugly?" queried Desmond.

"Well, not really ugly …" Tough pondered, "maybe a little smelly."

Desmond grimaced.

"Anyway, the next few weeks were quite uneventful, except that we all kept losing things. Nothing big went missing, just a little money, a good penknife, a nice book, that sort of thing. After a while we treated it as a joke. Nothing really valuable had vanished, so we put it down to our own forgetfulness or untidiness."

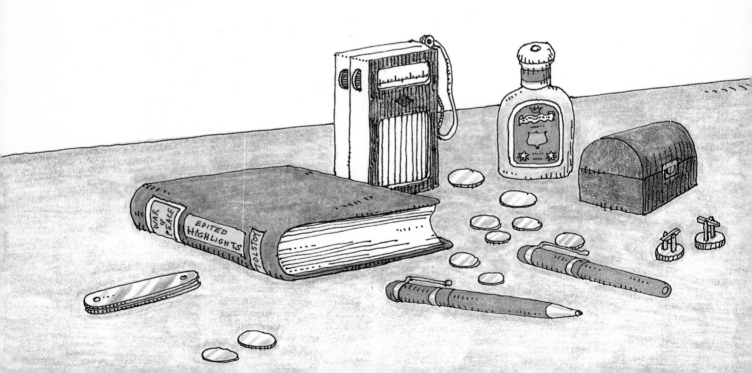

"But as time went by, I became more and more concerned about the way so many things were disappearing and I was convinced it all had something to do with Sneaky and his parcels home. I didn't have any proof that he'd been pilfering the stuff but I think he realised that I was on to him because he started being extra nice to me. Then I really knew he was up to something."

"I know just what you mean," said Desmond wisely. He studied the man outside and stroked his chin in a serious manner. "So what happened next?"

"I decided to set a trap for him," said Tough.

"Cor, Sneaky Ted!" Desmond grinned. Tough smiled.

"I left some money in my cabin," Tough went on, "and put a little bit of honey on it … just enough to attract the bees, so to speak. I memorised what I'd left and how it was set out, so, if anything was taken, I would know straight away.

"Later, as we were about to leave port, I nipped into my cabin to check on the cash. Sure enough, some of it was gone – not too much, nothing too noticeable – but some of it was gone all the same. I was sure Sneaky had swiped it and I knew exactly how to prove my theory with some concrete evidence."

"As they say at Scotland Yard," interrupted Desmond cheekily.

"As they say at Scotland Yard," Tough agreed, smiling.

"So when I went into the galley for some lunch, I went up to Sneaky and asked him if he could change some money. He didn't suspect a thing and went through his pockets to give me some change ... rather sticky coins ... honey money!"

"Wow!" gasped Desmond. "He gave you back your own money!"

"He certainly did," agreed Tough, "and he didn't even realise that I knew."

"What did you do then?" Desmond asked, settling down in a chair.

"I had to inform the Captain," Tough explained. "All I wanted was for Sneaky to be dismissed and everything to be returned. I talked to the Captain as soon as I could and he was a bit sad that Sneaky had turned out to be such a rotten bilge rat."

"Yeah – and a lousy, low-down, light-fingered layabout," sneered Desmond, making another face.

"Yes, that too," said Tough, a little taken aback.

There was a pause as Desmond inched forward, sensing that Tough was about to get to the really exciting part.

"Sneaky had just returned from his latest trip ashore," Tough carried on, "and he was on deck watching the crew cast off as I stood talking to the Captain. I noticed him looking at the skipper and me a couple of times, but we didn't know if he realised that we knew."

"So you didn't know if he knew that you knew and he didn't know that you knew what he knew … or did he know that …" thought Desmond aloud.

"Shut up, Desmond," said Tough with a laugh.

"Yes, Mon Kapitan," said Desmond with a salute. "Just thinking aloud, sir."

"Yes, I saw your lips move," said Tough, patting Desmond's head rather vigorously.

"Then, just as I finished talking to the skipper,
a heavy loading hook suspended from a swinging
boom came hurtling through the air. It was
heading straight for the skipper and it was going to
knock his block off!"

"Without thinking I leapt forward and pushed the Captain aside, then BANG! The hook hit me like a clap of thunder!"

"What a thump . . . for a moment or two everything went white. I knew I'd been hit and I knew it was going to hurt like blazes, but at that point I didn't feel a thing."

"You were in shock," said Desmond.

"I reckon I must have been," agreed Tough. "All I could think about was Sneaky McQueen. He'd been standing beside that hook. It didn't take a genius to work out that he'd flung the hook and that he'd meant it for me – to shut me up!"

"For ever and a day," said Desmond gravely, biting his lip.

"The rest of the crew stood around in amazement," said Tough. "They hadn't a clue what was going on. I walked slowly towards Sneaky. He looked terrified. I wasn't going to hurt him ... I was just going to hand him over to the skipper and get him off the ship."

"By now the side of my head really hurt … I could feel the blood dribbling down my face … but I was so angry that it just didn't seem to matter. As I got closer to Sneaky he began to back away, then suddenly he ran for the rail, jumped up and made to leap from the moving ship onto the quay."

"Making his escape!" yelled Desmond, getting rather excited.

"Exactly," replied Tough, "but in his haste he slipped and instead of jumping to safety he fell over the side. Now that was really dangerous, Desmond, because the ship was moving off and there wasn't much room between us and the quay."

"Crikey, Tough!" exclaimed Desmond, leaping to his feet. "Did Sneaky fall in? Did he get hurt?"

"Well, no . . ." said Tough. "When he fell he grabbed for the rail. He missed it but caught hold of one of the ropes instead. He was dangling there between the steel hull and the stone quay . . . and that, Desmond, isn't the safest place to be, even if you are Sneaky McQueen!"

Desmond stood with his mouth open. Tough closed it for him.

"I decided that the only thing to do was to rescue the wretch. I climbed over the rail and lowered myself down, holding on as best I could to the rail support."

"Like Tarzan," said Desmond, interrupting again.

"Not quite," smiled Tough. "It was a pretty tight spot, I can tell you, but I was able to jam my foot up against the quay and hold the hull of the ship away from the dock. Otherwise we would both have been squashed as flat as flounders! Gradually, I managed to help Sneaky climb up and onto the deck."

"For a while he just lay there panting and puffing, as white as a sail, then he pulled himself together and staggered off to his cabin. By the end of the afternoon I was bandaged up and he was ready to go. We had to take him with us for a bit but we dropped him off that evening just along the coast. We didn't even get our things back."

"Oh, no, Tough, really?" cried Desmond. "What happened to it all? I thought you said he mailed it all to somebody."

"Yes, that's what we thought too," said Tough. "But what he really did was as soon as he got ashore he ripped open his 'parcels' and flogged the stuff to any sleazy shark he could find."

"Cor," said Desmond. "He really was sneaky, wasn't he? I bet the crew were glad to see the back of him, even if they did have to polish their own shoes from then on!"

Desmond sat down and looked across at the window to see the man outside turn away from the café and stroll off along Wharf Alley. Suddenly Desmond felt rather sorry for Sneaky McQueen. He seemed such a sad and lonely character and, by the look of him, still a little smelly.

WHARF ALLEY

FANTAIL PUBLISHING
an Imprint of Puffin Enterprises.

Published by the Penguin Group,
27 Wrights Lane,
London W8 5TZ,
England.

First published 1989.

13579108642

014 0900225

Typesetting by Fullpoint Filmsetting Ltd.

Printed in Italy by
Printers srl – Trento.

Desmond looked up at Tough.

"But, Tough," he said, smiling mischievously, "what would you have done if Sneaky McQueen had come in just now and asked for a meal? Would you have served him?"

Tough paused and fiddled with his torn ear, then scooped Pip the cat up into his arms.

"Well, Desmond," he said at last, "I suppose I would have ... but I'd have checked my pockets and counted all the cutlery afterwards!"